The Golden Goose Book

The Golden Goose Book

A Fairy Tale Picture Book

Illustrated by
L. Leslie Brooke

With an afterword by
Neil Philip

CLARION BOOKS

NEW YORK

Clarion Books
a Houghton Mifflin Company imprint
215 Park Avenue South, New York, NY 10003

An Albion Book

Designer: Andrew Shoolbred
Project Manager: Elizabeth Wilkes

This edition of THE GOLDEN GOOSE BOOK has been newly originated
from Leslie Brooke's original watercolors and line drawings,
which are reproduced courtesy of the Brooke family. The book
was first published in 1905.

Library of Congress Cataloging-in-Publication Data

Brooke, L. Leslie (Leonard Leslie), 1862-1940.
  The golden goose book/L. Leslie Brooke.
    p.   cm.
  Summary: An illustrated collection of four traditional tales,
originally published in 1904
  ISBN 0-395-61303-5
  1. Fairy tales. [1. Fairy tales. 2. Folk lore.] I. Title.
PZ8.B6816Go 1992
398.2--dc20
[E]   91-26584
                                           CIP
                                           AC

00 10 9 8 7 6 5 4 3 2 1

Typesetting by York House Typographic, London
Color origination by Pressplan Reprographics Ltd, Watford
Printed and bound in Hong Kong by South China Printing Co.

Contents

The Golden Goose
8

The Story of the Three Bears
32

The Story of the Three Little Pigs
52

Tom Thumb
70

Afterword
93

The Golden Goose

There was once a man who had three sons, the youngest of whom was called the Simpleton. He was laughed at and despised and neglected on all occasions. Now it happened one day that the eldest son wanted to go into the forest, to hew wood, and his Mother gave him a beautiful cake and a bottle of wine to take with him, so that he might not suffer from hunger or thirst. When he came to the wood he met a little old grey man, who, bidding him good-day, said, "Give me a small piece of the cake in your wallet, and let me drink a mouthful of your wine; I am so hungry and thirsty." But the clever son answered, "If I were

to give you my cake and wine, I should have none for myself, so be off with you," and he left the little man standing there, and walked away. Hardly had he begun to cut down a tree, when his axe slipped and cut his arm, so that he had to go home at once and have the wound bound up. This was the work of the little grey man.

Thereupon the second son went into the wood, and the Mother gave him, as she had given to the eldest, a sweet cake and a bottle of wine. The little old man met him also, and begged for a small slice of cake and a drink of wine. But the second son spoke

out quite plainly. "What I give to you I lose myself – be off with you," and he left the little man standing there, and walked on. Punishment was not long in coming to him, for he had given but two strokes at a tree when he cut his leg so badly that he had to be carried home.

Then said the Simpleton, "Father, let me go into the forest and hew wood." But his Father answered him, "Your brothers have done themselves much harm, so as you understand nothing about wood-cutting you had better not try." But the Simpleton begged for so long that at last the Father said, "Well, go if you like; experience will soon make you wiser." To him the Mother gave a cake, but it was made with water and had been baked in the ashes, and with it she gave him a bottle of sour beer. When he came to the wood the little grey man met him also, and greeted him, and said, "Give me a slice of your cake and a drink from your bottle; I am so hungry and thirsty." The Simpleton replied, "I have only a cake that has been baked in the ashes, and some sour beer, but if that will satisfy you, let us sit down and eat together." So they sat themselves down, and as the Simpleton held out his food it became a rich cake, and the sour beer became good wine. So they ate and drank together, and when the meal was finished the little man said, "As you have a good heart and give so willingly a share of your own, I will grant you good luck. Yonder stands an old tree; hew it down, and in its roots you will find something." Saying this the old man took his departure, and off went the Simpleton and cut down the tree. When it fell, there among its roots sat a goose, with feathers of pure gold. He lifted her out, and carried her with him to an inn where he intended to stay the night.

Now the innkeeper had three daughters, who on seeing the goose were curious to know what wonderful kind of a bird it could be, and longed to have one of its golden feathers. The eldest daughter thought to herself, "Surely a chance will come for me to pull out one of those feathers"; and so when the Simpleton had gone out, she caught the goose by the wing. But there her hand stuck fast! Shortly afterwards the second daughter came, as she too was longing for a golden feather. She had hardly touched

her sister, however, when she also stuck fast. And lastly came the third daughter with the same object. At this the others cried out, "Keep off, for goodness' sake, keep off!" But she, not understanding why they told her to keep away, thought to herself, "If they go to the goose, why should not I?" and she sprang forwards, but as she touched her sister she too stuck fast, and pull as she might she could not get away; and thus they had all to pass the night beside the goose.

The next morning the Simpleton took the goose under his arm and went on his way, without troubling himself at all about the three girls who were hanging on to the bird. There they went, always running behind him, now to the right, now to the left, whichever way he chose to go. In the middle of the fields they met the parson, and when he saw the procession he called out,

"Shame on you, you naughty girls, why do you run after a young fellow in this way? Come, leave go!" With this he caught the youngest by the hand, and tried to pull her back, but when he touched her he found he could not get away, and he too must needs run behind. Then the sexton came along, and saw the parson following on the heels of the three girls. This so aston-ished him that he called out, "Hi! Sir Parson, whither away so fast? Do you forget that to-day we have a christening?" and ran after

him, and caught him by the coat, but he too remained sticking fast.

As the five now ran on, one behind the other, two labourers who were returning from the field with their tools, came along. The parson called out to them and begged that they would set him and the sexton free. No sooner had they touched the sexton, than they too had to hang on, and now there were seven running after the Simpleton and the goose.

In this way they came to a city where a King reigned who had an only daughter, who was so serious that no one could make her laugh. Therefore he had announced that whoever should make her laugh should have her for his wife. When the Simpleton heard this he went with his goose and his train before the Princess, and when she saw the seven people all running behind each other, she began to laugh, and she laughed and laughed till it seemed as though she could never stop. Thereupon the

Simpleton demanded her for his wife, but the King was not pleased at the thought of such a son-in-law, and he made all kinds of objections. He told the Simpleton that he must first bring him a man who could drink off a whole cellarful of wine. At once the Simpleton thought of the little grey man, who would be sure to help him, so off he went into the wood, and in the place where he had cut down the tree he saw a man sitting who looked most miserable. The Simpleton asked him what was the cause of his trouble.

"I have such a thirst," the man answered, "and I cannot quench it. I cannot bear cold water. I have indeed emptied a cask of wine, but what is a drop like that to a thirsty man?"

"In that case I can help you," said the Simpleton. "Just come with me and you shall be satisfied."

He led him to the King's cellar, and the man at once sat down in front of the great cask, and drank and drank till before a day was over he had drunk the whole cellarful of wine. Then the

L.L.B.

Simpleton demanded his bride again, but the King was angry that a mean fellow everyone called a Simpleton should win his daughter, and he made new conditions. Before giving him his daughter to wife he said that the Simpleton must find a man who would eat a whole mountain of bread. The Simpleton did not

stop long to consider, but went off straight to the wood. There in the same place as before sat a man who was buckling a strap tightly around him, and looking very depressed. He said, "I have eaten a whole ovenful of loaves, but what help is that when a man is as hungry as I am? I feel quite empty, and I must strap myself together if I am not to die of hunger."

The Simpleton was delighted on hearing this, and said, "Get up at once and come with me. I will give you enough to eat to satisfy your hunger."

He led him to the King, who meanwhile had ordered all the meal in the Kingdom to be brought together, and an immense mountain of bread baked from it. The man from the wood set to work on it, and in one day the whole mountain had disappeared.

For the third time the Simpleton demanded his bride, but yet again the King tried to put him off, and said that he must bring him a ship that would go both on land and water.

"If you are really able to sail such a ship," said he, "you shall at once have my daughter for your wife."

The Simpleton went into the wood, and there sat the little old grey man to whom he had given his cake.

"I have drunk for you, and I have eaten for you," said the little man, "and I will also give you the ship; all this I do for you because you were kind to me."

Then he gave the Simpleton a ship that went both on land and water, and when the King saw it he knew he could no longer keep

back his daughter. The wedding was celebrated, and after the King's death, the Simpleton inherited the Kingdom, and lived very happily ever after with his wife.

THE THREE BEARS

The Story of
the Three Bears

O nce upon a time there were Three Bears, who lived together in a house of their own, in a wood. One of them was a Little, Small, Wee Bear; and one was a Middle-sized Bear, and the other was a Great, Huge Bear. They had each a pot for their porridge; a little pot for the Little, Small, Wee Bear; and a middle-sized pot for the Middle Bear, and a great pot for the Great, Huge Bear. And they had each a chair to sit in; a little chair for the Little, Small, Wee Bear; and a middle-sized chair

for the Middle Bear, and a great chair for the Great, Huge Bear. And they had each a bed to sleep in; a little bed for the Little, Small, Wee Bear; and a middle-sized bed for the Middle Bear, and a great bed for the Great, Huge Bear.

One day, after they had made the porridge for their breakfast, and poured it into their porridge-pots, they walked out into the wood while the porridge was cooling, that they might not burn their mouths by beginning too soon to eat it. And while they were

walking, a little Girl called Goldenlocks came to the house. First she looked in at the window, and then she peeped in at the keyhole; and seeing nobody in the house, she turned the handle of the door. The door was not fastened, because the Bears were good Bears, who did nobody any harm, and never suspected that anybody would harm them. So Goldenlocks opened the door, and went in; and well pleased she was when she saw the porridge on the table. If she had been a thoughtful little Girl, she would have waited till the Bears came home, and then, perhaps, they would have asked her to breakfast; for they were good Bears – a little rough or so, as the manner of Bears is, but for all that very

good-natured and hospitable. But the porridge looked tempting, and she set about helping herself.

So first she tasted the porridge of the Great, Huge Bear, and that was too hot for her. And then she tasted the porridge of the Middle Bear, and that was too cold for her. And then she went to the porridge of the Little, Small, Wee Bear, and tasted that; and that was neither too hot nor too cold, but just right, and she liked it so well that she ate it all up.

Then Goldenlocks sat down in the chair of the Great, Huge Bear, and that was too hard for her. And then she sat down in the chair of the Middle Bear, and that was too soft for her. And then she sat down in the chair of the Little, Small, Wee Bear, and that was neither too hard nor too soft, but just right. So she seated herself in it, and there she sat till the bottom of the chair came out, and down she came plump upon the ground.

Then Goldenlocks went upstairs into the bed-chamber in which the three Bears slept. And first she lay down upon the bed of the Great, Huge Bear, but that was too high at the head for her.

And next she lay down upon the bed of the Middle Bear, and that was too high at the foot for her. And then she lay down upon the bed of the Little, Small, Wee Bear; and that was neither too high at the head nor at the foot, but just right. So she covered herself up comfortably, and lay there till she fell fast asleep.

By this time the Three Bears thought their porridge would be cool enough; so they came home to breakfast. Now Goldenlocks had left the spoon of the Great, Huge Bear standing in his porridge.

"SOMEBODY HAS BEEN AT MY PORRIDGE!"

said the Great, Huge Bear, in his great, rough, gruff voice. And when the Middle Bear looked at hers, she saw that the spoon was standing in it too.

"SOMEBODY HAS BEEN AT MY PORRIDGE!"

said the Middle Bear, in her middle voice. Then the Little, Small,

Wee Bear looked at his, and there was the spoon in the porridge-pot, but the porridge was all gone.

"SOMEBODY HAS BEEN AT MY PORRIDGE, AND HAS EATEN IT ALL UP!"

said the Little, Small, Wee Bear, in his little, small, wee voice.

Upon this the Three Bears, seeing that someone had entered their house, and eaten up the Little, Small, Wee Bear's breakfast, began to look about them. Now Goldenlocks had not put the hard cushion straight when she rose from the chair of the Great, Huge Bear.

"SOMEBODY HAS BEEN SITTING IN MY CHAIR!"

said the Great, Huge Bear, in his great, rough, gruff voice.

And Goldenlocks had squashed down the soft cushion of the Middle Bear.

"SOMEBODY HAS BEEN SITTING IN MY CHAIR!"

said the Middle Bear, in her middle voice.

And you know what Goldenlocks had done to the third chair.

"SOMEBODY HAS BEEN SITTING IN MY CHAIR,
AND HAS SAT THE BOTTOM OUT OF IT!"

said the Little, Small, Wee Bear, in his little, small, wee voice.

Then the Three Bears thought it necessary that they should make further search; so they went upstairs into their bed-chamber. Now Goldenlocks had pulled the pillow of the Great, Huge Bear out of its place.

"SOMEBODY HAS BEEN LYING IN MY BED!"

said the Great, Huge Bear, in his great, rough, gruff voice.

And Goldenlocks had pulled the bolster of the Middle Bear out of its place.

"SOMEBODY HAS BEEN LYING IN MY BED!"

said the Middle Bear, in her middle voice.

And when the Little, Small, Wee Bear came to look at his bed, there was the bolster in its place; and the pillow in its place upon the bolster; and upon the pillow was the head of Goldenlocks – which was not in its place, for she had no business there.

"SOMEBODY HAS BEEN LYING IN MY BED – AND HERE SHE IS!"

said the Little, Small, Wee Bear, in his little, small, wee voice.

Goldenlocks had heard in her sleep the great, rough, gruff voice of the Great, Huge Bear, and the middle voice of the Middle Bear, but it was only as if she had heard someone speaking in a dream. But when she heard the little, small, wee voice of the Little, Small, Wee Bear, it was so sharp, and so shrill, that it awakened her at once. Up she started; and when she saw the

Three Bears on one side of the bed she tumbled herself out at the other, and ran to the window. Now the window was open, because the Bears, like good, tidy Bears, as they were, always opened their bed-chamber window when they got up in the morning. Out Goldenlocks jumped, and ran away as fast as she could run – never looking behind her; and what happened to her afterwards I cannot tell. But the Three Bears never saw anything more of her.

THE STORY OF
THE
THREE LITTLE
PIGS

The Story of
the Three Little Pigs

O nce upon a time there was an old Sow with three little Pigs, and as she had not enough to keep them, she sent them out to seek their fortune. The first that went off met a Man with a bundle of straw, and said to him, "Please, Man, give me that straw to build me a house"; which the Man did, and the little Pig built a house with it. Presently came along a Wolf, and knocked at the door, and said, "Little Pig, little Pig, let me come in."

To which the Pig answered, "No, no, by the hair of my chinny chin chin."

"Then I'll huff and I'll puff, and I'll blow your house in!" said the Wolf. So he huffed and he puffed, and he blew the house in, and ate up the little Pig.

The second Pig met a Man with a bundle of furze, and said, "Please, Man, give me that furze to build a house"; which the Man did, and the Pig built his house. Then along came the Wolf and said, "Little Pig, little Pig, let me come in."

"No, no, by the hair of my chinny chin chin."

"Then I'll puff and I'll huff, and I'll blow your house in!" So he huffed and he puffed, and he puffed and he huffed, and at last he blew the house down, and ate up the second little Pig.

The third little Pig met a Man with a load of bricks, and said, "Please, Man, give me those bricks to build a house with"; so the Man gave him the bricks, and he built his house with them. So the Wolf came, as he did to the other little Pigs, and said, "Little Pig, little Pig, let me come in."

"No, no, by the hair of my chinny chin chin."

"Then I'll huff and I'll puff, and I'll blow your house in."

Well, he huffed and he puffed, and he huffed and he puffed, and he puffed and he huffed; but he could *not* get the house down. When he found that he could not, with all his huffing and puffing, blow the house down, he said, "Little Pig, I know where there is a nice field of turnips."

"Where?" said the little Pig.

"Oh, in Mr. Smith's home-field; and if you will be ready to-morrow morning, I will call for you, and we will go together and get some for dinner."

"Very well," said the little Pig, "I will be ready. What time do you mean to go?"

"Oh, at six o'clock."

Well, the little Pig got up at five, and got the turnips and was home again before six. When the Wolf came he said, "Little Pig, are you ready?"

"Ready!" said the little Pig, "I have been and come back again, and got a nice pot-full for dinner."

The Wolf felt very angry at this, but thought that he would be *up* to the little Pig somehow or other; so he said, "Little Pig, I know where there is a nice apple-tree."

"Where?" said the Pig.

"Down at Merry-garden," replied the Wolf; "and if you will not deceive me I will come for you, at five o'clock to-morrow, and we will go together and get some apples."

Well, the little Pig woke at four the next morning, and bustled up, and went off for the apples, hoping to get back before the Wolf came; but he had farther to go, and had to climb the tree, so that just as he was coming down from it, he saw the Wolf coming, which, as you may suppose, frightened him very much. When the Wolf came up he said, "Little Pig, what! are you here before me? Are they nice apples?"

"Yes, very," said the little Pig; "I will throw you down one." And he threw it so far that, while the Wolf was gone to pick it up, the little Pig jumped down and ran home.

The next day the Wolf came again, and said to the little Pig, "Little Pig, there is a Fair in the Town this afternoon: will you go?"

"Oh, yes," said the Pig, "I will go; what time shall you be ready?"

"At three," said the Wolf.

So the little Pig went off before the time, as usual, and got to the Fair, and bought a butter churn, and was on his way home with it when he saw the Wolf coming. Then he could not tell what to do. So he got into the churn to hide, and in doing so turned it round, and it began to roll, and rolled down the hill with the Pig inside it, which frightened the Wolf so much that he ran home without going to the Fair.

L.L.B.

He went to the little Pig's house, and told him how frightened he had been by a great round thing which came down the hill past him.

Then the little Pig said, "Hah! I frightened you, did I? I had been to the Fair and bought a butter churn, and when I saw you I got into it, and rolled down the hill."

Then the Wolf was very angry indeed, and declared he *would* eat up the little Pig, and that he would get down the chimney after him.

When the little Pig saw what he was about, he hung on the pot full of water, and made up a blazing fire, and, just as the Wolf was coming down, took off the cover of the pot, and in fell the Wolf. And the little Pig put on the cover again in an instant, boiled him up, and ate him for supper, and lived happy ever after.

Tom Thumb

Long ago, in the merry days of good King Arthur, there lived a ploughman and his wife. They were very poor, but would have been contented and happy if only they could have had a little child. One day, having heard of the great fame of the magician Merlin, who was living at the Court of King Arthur, the wife persuaded her husband to go and tell him of their trouble. Having arrived at the Court, the man besought Merlin with tears in his eyes to give them a child, saying that they would

be quite content even though it should be no bigger than his thumb. Merlin determined to grant the request, and what was the countryman's astonishment to find when he reached home that his wife had a son, who, wonderful to relate, was no bigger than his father's thumb!

The parents were now very happy, and the christening of the little fellow took place with great ceremony. The Fairy Queen, attended by all her company of elves, was present at the feast. She

kissed the little child, and, giving it the name of Tom Thumb, told
her fairies to fetch the tailors of her Court, who dressed her little
godson according to her orders. His hat was made of a beautiful
oak leaf, his shirt of a fine spider's web, and his hose and doublet
were of thistledown, his stockings were made with the rind of a
delicate green apple, and the garters were two of the finest little
hairs imaginable, plucked from his mother's eyebrows, while his
shoes were made of the skin of a little mouse. When he was thus

dressed, the Fairy Queen kissed him once more, and, wishing him all good luck, flew off with the fairies to her Court.

As Tom grew older, he became very amusing and full of tricks, so that his mother was afraid to let him out of her sight. One day,

while she was making a batter pudding, Tom stood on the edge of the bowl, with a lighted candle in his hand, so that she might see that the pudding was made properly. Unfortunately, however, when her back was turned, Tom fell into the bowl, and his mother, not missing him, stirred him up in the pudding, tied it in a cloth, and put it into the pot. The batter filled Tom's mouth, and prevented him from calling out, but he had no sooner felt the hot water, than he kicked and struggled so much that the pudding

jumped about in the pot, and his mother, thinking the pudding was bewitched, was nearly frightened out of her wits. Pulling it out of the pot, she ran with it to her door, and gave it to a tinker who was passing. He was very thankful for it, and looked forward to having a better dinner than he had enjoyed for many a long day. But his pleasure did not last long, for, as he was getting over a stile, he happened to sneeze very hard, and Tom, who had been quite quiet inside the pudding for some time, called out at the top

of his little voice, "Hallo, Pickens!" This so terrified the tinker that he flung away the pudding, and ran off as fast as he could. The pudding was all broken to pieces by the fall, and Tom crept out, covered with batter, and ran home to his mother, who had been

looking everywhere for him, and was delighted to see him again. She gave him a bath in a cup, which soon washed off all the pudding, and he was none the worse for his adventure.

A few days after this, Tom accompanied his mother when she went into the fields to milk the cows, and, fearing he might be blown away by the wind, she tied him to a sow-thistle with a little piece of thread. While she was milking, a cow came by, bit off the thistle, and swallowed up Tom. Poor Tom did not like her big

teeth, and called out loudly, "Mother, Mother!" "But where are you, Tommy, my dear Tommy?" cried out his mother, wringing her hands. "Here, Mother," he shouted, "inside the red cow's mouth!" And, saying that, he began to kick and scratch till the poor cow was nearly mad, and at length tumbled him out of her mouth. On seeing this, his mother rushed to him, caught him in her arms, and carried him safely home.

Some days after this, his father took him to the fields a-ploughing, and gave him a whip, made of barley straw, with which to drive the oxen; but little Tom was soon lost in a furrow. An eagle seeing him, picked him up and flew with him to the top of a hill where stood a giant's castle. The giant put him at once into his mouth, intending to swallow him up, but Tom made such a great disturbance when he got inside that the monster was soon

glad to get rid of him, and threw him far away into the sea. But he was not drowned, for he had scarcely touched the water before he was swallowed by a large fish, which was shortly afterwards captured and brought to King Arthur, as a present, by the fisherman. When the fish was opened, everyone was astonished at finding Tom inside. He was at once carried to the King, who made him his Court dwarf.

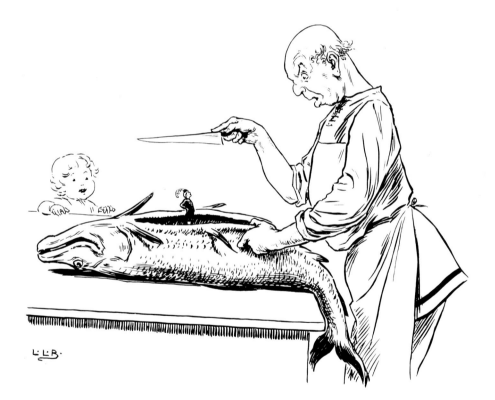

Long time he lived in jollity,
Beloved of the Court,
And none like Tom was so esteemed
Amongst the better sort.

The Queen was delighted with the little boy, and made him dance a gaillard on her left hand. He danced so well that King Arthur gave him a ring, which he wore round his waist like a girdle.

Tom soon began to long to see his parents again, and begged the King to allow him to go home for a short time. This was readily permitted, and the King told him he might take with him as much money as he could carry.

And so away goes lusty Tom,
With three pence at his back –
A heavy burthen which did make
His very bones to crack.

He had to rest more than a hundred times by the way, but, after two days and two nights, he reached his father's house in safety. His mother saw him coming, and ran out to meet him, and there was great rejoicing at his arrival. He spent three happy days at home, and then set out for the Court once more.

Shortly after his return, he one day displeased the King, so, fearing the royal anger, he crept into an empty flower-pot, where he lay for a long time. At last he ventured to peep out, and, seeing a fine large butterfly on the ground close by, he stole out of his hiding-place, jumped on its back, and was carried up into the air.

The King and nobles all strove to catch him, but at last poor Tom fell from his seat into a watering-pot, in which he was almost drowned, only luckily the gardener's child saw him, and pulled him out. The King was so pleased to have him safe once more that he forgot to scold him, and made much of him instead.

Tom afterwards lived many years at Court, one of the best beloved of King Arthur's knights.

> *Thus he at tilt and tournament*
> *Was entertainèd so,*
> *That all the rest of Arthur's knights*
> *Did him much pleasure show.*
> *With good Sir Launcelot du Lake,*
> *Sir Tristram and Sir Guy,*
> *Yet none compared to brave Tom Thumb*
> *In acts of chivalry.*

Afterword

Leslie Brooke is one of the most important children's illustrators of the twentieth century. The verve of his line and the robustness of his humor quickly established his reputation as, in the words of Maurice Sendak, "a spiritual descendant of Caldecott."

He was born Leonard Leslie Brooke in Birkenhead, Cheshire, England, on September 24, 1862, and studied art at Birkenhead Art School and subsequently at the St. John's Wood Art School and the Royal Academy Art Schools in London.

On completing his training, he began to undertake book illustrations for various publishers. In 1891 he took over from Walter Crane as the regular illustrator of books by Mrs. Molesworth, one of the leading children's writers of the day.

The book which made his name, and linked him for the rest of his career with the firm of Warne, who published all his important books, was *The Nursery Rhyme Book*, edited by Andrew Lang. This glorious collection of traditional rhymes contained over a hundred black-and-white drawings of unusual energy, wit, and lyricism. The book was a great success, partly no doubt because of Lang's prestigious name on the title page, though it was Leslie Brooke himself who had selected the rhymes.

Warne followed up *The Nursery Rhyme Book* with two selections of nonsense poems by Edward Lear, *The Pelican Chorus* and *The Jumblies*, which were the first and are possibly still the best attempt by another hand to illustrate Lear's zany and oddly wistful rhymes. For these books, which were later combined into one volume, Leslie Brooke was allowed to supplement his line drawings with color plates.

The mixture of color and black-and-white illustrations in the Lear books was repeated in even more lavish abundance in Leslie Brooke's *The Golden Goose Book* (1905) and *Ring O' Roses* (1922), which

Virginia Haviland, first Head of the Children's Book Section of the Library of Congress, has described as "irresistible picture-book treatments of traditional material that will endlessly enrich our literature for small children." These two books alone would guarantee Leslie Brooke's lasting fame as an illustrator, brimming as they are with vitality and movement and endless amusing and cunning detail. Fortunately, virtually all the artwork has survived, and consequently can now benefit from all the advantages of modern color reproduction, to show more clearly than ever before the sensitivity as well as the boldness of Leslie Brooke's work.

The twinkling comedy of the Johnny Crow books — *Johnny Crow's Garden* (1903), *Johnny Crow's Party* (1907), and *Johnny Crow's New Garden* (1935) — took a final twist when, in a joke silently appreciated by all the Brooke family, the funeral arrangements on Leslie Brooke's death on May 1, 1941 were overseen by the firm of J. Crowe and Sons.

Leslie Brooke's work directly descends from the great illustrators who preceded him, Randolph Caldecott, Walter Crane, and Kate Greenaway, and traces of all three can be seen in his work, as can the influence of Sir John Tenniel, whose drawings Brooke often copied as a child. Among his contemporaries, the most meaningful comparison is probably with Beatrix Potter, whose *The Tale of Peter Rabbit* was published by Warne at Brooke's recommendation. As Joyce Irene Whalley and Tessa Rose Chester put it in their authoritative *History of Children's Book Illustration*, "There were few other picture-book artists in the first twenty years of this century comparable to Beatrix Potter. The only one of her standard who could challenge her in wit and skill and who shared her concern for the integration of word and picture, was L. Leslie Brooke." In the work of Brooke, as of Potter, there is always a direct appeal to the child reader. As for his own influence, it is hard to imagine Maurice Sendak's *Alligators All Around* without *Johnny Crow's Garden*, or Janet and Allan Ahlberg's *Each Peach Pear Plum* without *The Golden Goose Book* and *Ring O' Roses*.

Leslie Brooke's reputation has always been greater in the United States than in his native Britain, largely due to the enthusiastic championship of his work by Anne Carroll Moore, doyenne of children's librarians, and Bertha Mahony Miller, founding editor of the influential journal *The Horn Book*, which devoted its May 1941 issue to an appreciation of Brooke's work. Anne Carroll Moore, Director of Work

with Children in the New York Public Library, tirelessly promoted his books, elevating Johnny Crow, as her biographer Frances Clarke Sayers has observed, to "a folk hero among the picture-book set."

Anne Carroll Moore and Leslie Brooke became friends, and she describes their first meeting in a 1921 letter to her niece Rachel: "You would have loved both the home and the studio, everything was so *real*. Mr. Brooke and I literally fell into one another's arms and he wants to give me for myself one of his originals." Leslie Brooke's letters to Anne

Carroll Moore record some of his own artistic principles and influences. In a letter dated September 2, 1941, he quotes W. H. Hunt's advice, "draw firm and be jolly," before going on to discuss the grace and economy of draftsmanship that lie at the root of Randolph Caldecott's, and Leslie Brooke's, greatness: "to see how instinctive the inspiration of the very best type of picture book is, it is worth looking at the very first draft by Caldecott of his *House That Jack Built*. . . . It is just a series of scribbles but implicit in each scrawl can clearly be found the very dog, cat, rat, etc., that has become classic."

Looking at the exquisite new reproductions of Leslie Brooke's subtle watercolors, and admiring once again the clarity and expressiveness of his line drawings, one cannot but agree with Elizabeth Nesbitt's judgment in Virginia Haviland's *Children's Literature: Views and Reviews* that, despite all the marvelous picture books that have appeared in recent years, "the standards of conception and execution set by Randolph Caldecott and Leslie Brooke have not been surpassed."

Neil Philip
PRINCES RISBOROUGH
1992